Here Lies

preceded by

Indian Culture

T0001937

ANTONIN ARTAUD

HERE LIES

PRECEDED BY

INDIAN CULTURE

TRANSLATED AND WITH NOTES BY
CLAYTON ESHLEMAN

EDITED AND WITH AN AFTERWORD BY
STEPHEN BARBER

DIAPHANES

La Culture Indienne

INDIAN CULTURE

Je suis venu au Mexique prendre contact avec la
    Terre Rouge
et elle pue comme elle embaume ;
elle sent bon comme elle puait.

Cafre d'urine de la pente d'un vagin dur,
et qui se refuse quand on le prend.

Camphre urinaire de l'éminence d'un vagin mort,
et qui vous soufflette quand on l'étend,

quand on mire du haut du Mirador du Pitre,
tombe cloutée du père affreux,

le trou à creux, l'âcre trou creux, où bout le cycle
    des poux rouges,
cycle des poux solaires rouges,
tout blancs dans le lacis des veines de l'un deux.

Qui ça deux, et lequel des deux ?
Qui, les deux ?
au temps
septante fois maudit
où l'homme
                    se croisant lui-même
naissait fils

I came to Mexico to make contact with the
    Red Earth
and it stinks the same way that it embalms;
it smells good the same way that it stank.

Kaffir of urine from the slope of a tough vagina,
which when we grab it refuses to give.

Urinary camphor from the bulge of a dead vagina,
which smacks us when we spread it out,

when we eye, from the height of the Clown's Mirador,
the ghastly father's hobnailed tomb,

the hollowed hole, acrid hollow hole, where the
    cycle of red lice boils,
cycle of solar red lice,
all white in the veiny network of the one two.

Who that two, and which one of the two?
Who, the two?
in the age
seventy times cursed
when man
             crossing himself
was being born son

de sa sodomie
sur son propre cu
endurci.
Pourquoi deux d'eux,
et pourquoi de DEUX ?

Pitre affreux de père mimire,
immonde pitri parasite, dans creux mamiche retiré
     du feu !

Car les soleils qui passent tout ronds
ne sont rien auprès du pied bot,
de l'immense articulation
de la vieille jambe gangrène,
vieille jambe ossuaire gangrène,
où mûrit un bouclier d'os,

la levée souterraine, guerrière,
des boucliers de tous les os.

Qu'est-ce à dire ?

Ça veut dire que papa-mama n'encule plus le
     pédéraste inné,
l'immonde boutis des partouses chrétiennes,
interlope entre ji et cri,
contracté en
                    jiji-cricri,

et ça veut dire que la guerre
remplacera le père-mère

of his sodomy
on his own callused
butt.
Why two of them,
and why of TWO?

Ghastly clown of the pusseying father,*
filthy parasitic clone, in the hollow mamuffin*
    pulled out of the fire!

For the suns swallowed whole
are nothing compared to the clubfoot,
of the immense articulation
of old leg gangrene,
old boneyard leg gangrene,
where a shield of bones is ripening,

the warlike, underground uprising
of the shields of all the bones.

What does it mean?

It means that daddy-mommy* no longer buggers
    the innate pederast,
the filthy tusk holes* of Christian fuckfests,
interloper between ji and cry,
contracted in
                    jiji-crycry,

and it means that war
will replace the father-mother

9

là où le cu faisait barrière
contre la peste nourricière
de la Terre Rouge enterrée
sous le cadavre du guerrier
                    mort
pour n'avoir pas voulu passer
par le périple du serpent
qui se mord la queue par devant
cependant que papa-maman
lui mettent le derrière en sang.

Et qu'à y regarder de près,
dans la tranche tuméfiée de la jambe,
du vieux fémur couperosé
tombent
                    ça pue
                    et ça puait ;
et resurgit le vieux guerrier
de la cruauté insurgée,
de l'indicible cruauté
de vivre et de n'avoir pas d'être
qui puisse vous justifier ;
et tombent
dans le trou ancré
de la terre vue de haut, et en perce,
tous les bouts de langue éclairés,
et qui un jour se crurent âmes,
n'étant même pas des volontés ;

there where the butt raised a barrier
against the foster plague
of the Red Earth buried
under the corpse of the warrior
                    dead
for having refused to pass
through the periplus of the serpent
biting its tail from in front
while daddy-mommy
make his buttocks bloody.

And if scrutinizing closely,
in the tumified slice of leg,
from the old blotched thighbone
there fall
                    it stinks
                    and it stank;
and there resurges the old warrior
of insurgent cruelty,
of the unspeakable cruelty
of living and not having a being
who could justify you;
and there fall
into the anchored hole
of the earth seen from above, and abroach,
all the tips of lit-up tongue,
and which one day believed themselves souls,
not even being wills;

montent
tous les éclairs
de la schlague de ma main morte,
contre la langue soulevée,

et les sexes de volonté,

qui sont à peine des mots jetés,
lesquels n'ont pas pu prendre d'être ;

mais tombent mieux que des soleils
rejetés,
dans la cave où s'entretuaient
papa-maman
et pédéraste,
le fils d'avant que ça puait.

Quand l'âne solaire se croyait bon !

Et où était le ciel dans son rond ?

Où l'on était,
              dehors,
tout con
de sentir le ciel
                  dans son con,

sans rien qui pût faire barrière contre
    le vide,
où
pas de fond
et pas d'aplomb,
et pas de face,
ni de haut,
et où tout vous rapplique au fond,
quand on est droit tout de son long.

there rise
all the lightnings
from the flogging of my dead hand,
against the tongue in revolt,

and the sexes of will,

which are barely flung words,
that could not snag being;

but fall better than rejected
suns
into the cellar where, killing each other,
were daddy-mommy
and pederast,
the son from before it stank.

When the solar donkey believed himself good!

And where was the sky in its round?

Where one was,
                outside,
completely cunt
from feeling the sky
                in his cunt,

without anything that could raise a barrier against
    the void,
where
no bottom
and no upright
and no face,
nor top,
and where all hustles back to you at the bottom,
when one is all his length straight.

CI-GÎT

HERE LIES

Moi, Antonin Artaud, je suis mon fils, mon père,
    ma mère,
               et moi ;
niveleur du périple imbécile où s'enferre
    l'engendrement
le périple papa-maman
             et l'enfant,
suie du cu de la grand-maman,
beaucoup plus que du père-mère.

Ce qui veut dire qu'avant maman et papa
qui n'avaient ni père ni mère,
          dit-on,
et où donc les auraient-ils pris,
          eux,
quand ils devinrent ce conjoint
          unique
que ni l'épouse ni l'époux
n'a pu voir assis ou debout,
avant cet improbable trou
que l'esprit se cherche pour nous,
               pour nous
dégoûter un peu plus de nous,
était ce corps inemployable,
fait de viande et de sperme fou,
ce corps pendu, d'avant les poux,
suant sur l'impossible table
du ciel
son odeur calleuse d'atome,
sa rogomeuse odeur d'abject
détritus

Me, Antonin Artaud, I am my son, my father,
    my mother,
                and me;
leveler of the imbecilic periplus where begetting
    impales itself,
the daddy-mommy periplus
                and the child,
soot from grandma's ass,
much more than father-mother's.

Which means that before mommy and daddy
who had neither father nor mother,
                it is said,
and where indeed would they have got them,
                they,
when they became this unique
                conjunct
no husband nor wife
could have seen sit or stand,
before this improbable hole
the spirit feels out for us,
                to fill us
with a little more self-disgust,
was this unemployable body,
made of meat and mad sperm,
this body hanged, from before lice,
sweating on the impossible table
of heaven
its callous atom odor,
its croupous odor of abject
detritus

éjecté du somme
de l'Inca mutilé des doigts

qui pour idée avait un bras
mais n'avait de main qu'une paume
morte, d'avoir perdu ses doigts
à force de tuer de rois.

ejected from the snooze
of the finger-mutilated Inca

who for an idea had an arm
but had as a hand only a dead
palm, having lost his fingers
by dint of killing kings.

Avant donc DIZJE tout cela,
était la radineuse,
était cette râleuse

cause du ventre
au ciel bouffant

et qui chemina,
la hideuse,
7 fois 7 ans,
7 trilliards d'ans,
suivant la piteuse
arithmétique
de l'antique goémantie,

jusqu'à ce que des mamelles en sang
éjectées
de la cendre creuse
qui suinte du firmament
lui jaillît enfin cet enfant
maudit de l'homme
et de l'enfer même,

mais que dieu
plus laid que Satan

élut pour faire
la pige à l'homme

et il l'appela être
cet enfant

Hence SEZ-I before all that,
was the stingy old bag,
this grouchy nag

cause of the belly
with its bouffant heaven

who trudged along
— the hideous hag —
7 times 7 years,
7 trilliard years,
following the piteous
arithmetic
of ancient geomancy,

until from blood-smeared breasts
ejected
from the hollow ash
seeping from the firmament
spurted forth at last this child
cursed by man
and by hell itself,

but whom god
uglier than Satan

elected to take
the shine out of man

and he called him being
this child

qui avait un sexe
entre ses dents.

Car un autre enfant
était vrai,
était réel,

sans grand-maman
qui pût l'élire
de tout son ventre,

de toute sa fesse
de chien puant,

sorti seul
de la main en sang
de l'Inca mutilé des doigts.

who had a sex organ
between his teeth.

For another child
was true,
was real,

with no grandma
who could elect him
with her whole belly,

with her whole buttock
of a stinking dog,

emerged alone
from the finger-mutilated Inca's
blood-smeared hand.

Ici faisant marcher les cymbales de fer
je prends la basse route à gouges
dans l'œsophage de l'œil droit

sous la tombe du plexus roide
qui sur la route fait un coude
pour dégager l'enfant de droit.

        nuyon kidi
        nuyon kadan
        nuyon kada
        tara dada i i
        ota papa
        ota strakman
        tarma strapido
        ota rapido
        ota brutan
        otargugido
        ote krutan

Car je fus Inca mais pas roi.

        kilzi
        trakilzi
        faildor
        bara bama
        baraba
        mince

etretili

Here working the iron cymbals
I take the low road of gouges
in the esophagus of the right eye

under the tomb of the rigid plexus
which on the road sharply flexes
to extricate the child by right.

> **nuyon kidi**
> **nuyon kadan**
> **nuyon kada**
> **tara dada i i**
> **ota papa**
> **ota strakman**
> **tarma strapido**
> **ota rapido**
> **ota brutan**
> **otargugido**
> **ote krutan**

For I was Inca but not king.

> **kilzi**
> **trakilzi**
> **faildor**
> **bara bama**
> **baraba**
> **mince**

etretili

TILI
te pince
dans la *falzourchte*
de tout or,
dans la déroute
de tout corps.

Et il n'y avait ni soleil ni personne,
pas un être en avant de moi,
non, pas d'être qui me tutoyât.

Je n'avais que quelques fidèles qui ne cessaient de
mourir pour moi.

Quand ils furent trop morts pour vivre,
je ne vis plus que des haineux,
les mêmes qui guignaient leur place,
en combattant à côté d'eux,
trop lâches pour lutter contre eux.

Mais qui les avait vus ?

Personne.

Myrmidons de la Perséphone
Infernale,
microbes de tout geste en creux,
glaires pitreux d'une loi morte,
kystes de qui se viole entre eux,
langues de l'avaricieux
forceps
gratté sur son urine
même,
latrines de la morte osseuse,
que taraude toujours la même
vigueur
morne,
du même feu,

TILI
tweeks you
in the *pantabazooms*˙
of all gold,
in the rout
of all body.

And there was no sun, no one,
not a single being ahead of me,
no, no being on a first name basis with me.

I had only a few faithful who didn't cease dying
    for me.

When they were too dead to live,
I saw only the hateful,
the same who coveted their place,
while battling beside them,
too cowardly to struggle against them.

But who had seen them?

No one.

Myrmidons of the Infernal
                Persephone,
microbes of each concave gesture,
buffoonic phlegm of a dead law,
cysts of who rapes herself among them,
tongues of the avaricious
forceps
scraped on her urine
                itself,
latrines of the bony dead woman,
always screw-cut with the same
bleak
                vigor,
of the same fire,

            dont l'antre
innovateur d'un nœud
                terrible,

mis en clôture
de vie mère,

est la vipère
de mes œufs.

                    whose lair
innovator of a terrible
                    knot,

encloistered
with mother life,

is the viper (father life)*
of my eggs.

Car c'est la fin qui est le commencement.
Et cette fin
est celle-même
qui élimine
tous les moyens.

For it is the end which is the beginning.
And this end
is the very one
that eliminates
all means.

Et maintenant,
                vous tous, les êtres,
j'ai à vous dire que vous m'avez toujours fait caguer.
                Et allez vous faire
                engruper
                la moumoute
                de la parpougnête,
                morpions
                de l'éternité.

And now,
                    all of you, beings,
I have to tell you that you've always made me crap.
                    So go get
                    the quim-wig
                    for your scrubby grope-slope*
                    croupswarmed,
                    you crab lice
                    of eternity.

Je ne me rencontrerai pas une fois de plus avec des
    êtres qui avalèrent le clou de vie.

Et je me rencontrai un jour avec les êtres qui
        avalèrent le clou de vie,
— sitôt que j'eus perdu ma mamelle matrice,

et l'être me tordit sous lui,
et dieu me reversa à elle.
                    (LE SALIGAUD.)

Not once more will I be found with beings who
swallowed the nail of life.

And one day I found myself with the beings who
swallowed the nail of life
— as soon as I lost my matrix mamma,

and the being twisted me under him,
and god poured me back to her.
(THE MOTHERFUCKER)

C'est ainsi que l'on
tira de moi
papa et maman
et la friture de ji en
Cri
au sexe (centre)
du grand étranglement,
d'où fut tiré ce croi

                    sement de la bière

(morte)
et de la matière,
qui donna vie
à Jizo-cri
quand de la fiente de
             moi mort

fut tiré
le sang
dont se dore

          toute vie usurpée
          dehors.

This is how
daddy and mommy were
pulled out of me
and the dish of fried ji in
Cry
at the sex organ (center)
of the great strangling,
from which was pulled this cros
                        seeding of the coffin
(dead)
and of matter
which gave life
to Jizo-cry
when from the guano of
            me dead
was drawn
the blood
with which each life
                usurped outside gilds
                itself.

C'est ainsi que :
le grand secret de la culture indienne
est de ramener le monde à zéro,
toujours,

mais plutôt
1°   trop tard que plus tôt,

2°   ce qui veut dire
     plus tôt
     que trop tôt,

3°   ce qui veut dire que le plus tard ne
     peut revenir que si plus tôt a mangé
     trop tôt,

4°   ce qui veut dire que dans le temps
     le plus tard
     est ce qui précède
     et le trop tôt
     et le plus tôt,

5°   et que si précipité soit plus tôt
     le trop tard

     qui ne dit pas mot
     est toujours là,

     qui point par point
     désemboîte
     tous les plus tôt.

And* that is how:
the great secret of Indian culture
is to lead the world back to zero,
always,

but rather
        1°   too late than sooner,

        2°   which means
               sooner
               than too soon,

        3°   which means that the latest can
               come back only if sooner has eaten
               too soon,

        4°   which means that in time
               the latest
               is that which comes before
               and the too soon
               and the sooner,

        5°   and that however hurried sooner
               may be even later

               which does not say a word
               is always there,

               which point by point
               disencases
               all the sooners.

COMMENTAIRE

Ils vinrent, tous les saligauds,
après le grand désemboîtage,
manifesté de bas en haut.

       1°   om-let cadran

(ceci chuchoté :)

    Vous ne saviez pas ça
    que l'état
               ŒUF
    était l'état
    anti-Artaud
    par excellence
    et que pour empoisonner Artaud
    il n'y a rien
    de tel que de battre
    une bonne omelette
    dans les espaces
    visant le point
    gélatineux

COMMENTARY

They came, all the motherfuckers,
after the great disencasement
manifested from bottom to top.

      1° om-let dial

                           (this whispered:)

      You didn't know this
      that the EGG
                  state
      was the anti-
      Artaud state
      par excellence
      and that to poison Artaud
      there is nothing
      like whisking up
      a good omelette
      in the spaces
      aiming at the gelatinous
      point

qu'Artaud
cherchant l'homme à faire
a fui
comme une peste horrible
et c'est ce point
qu'on remet en lui,
rien de tel qu'une bonne omelette
fourrée poison, cyanure, câpres,
transmise par l'air à son cadavre
pour désarticuler Artaud
dans l'anathème de ses os
PENDUS SUR L'INTERNE CADASTRE.

et 2°   **palaoulette tirant
largalalouette te titrant**

3°   **tuban titi tarftan** de la tête et de la
tête te visant

4°   **lomonculus du frontal poince
et de la pince te putant**

il bascule au patron puant,
ce capitaliste arrogant
des limbes
nageant vers le recollement
du père-mère au sexe enfant
afin de vider le corps entière,
entièrement de sa matière
et d'y mettre à la place, qui ?
Celui que l'être et le néant
fit,
comme l'on donne à faire pipi.

which Artaud
searching for the man to be made
has fled
like a horrible plague
and it is this point
they put back in him,
nothing like a good poison
cyanide and capers stuffed omelette,
transmitted by the air to his cadaver
to disarticulate Artaud
in the anathema of his bones
HANGED ON THE INTERNAL CADASTRE.

and 2° **nolarking* extricating
lotsamalarkey titrating you**

3° **tuban titi tarftan** of the head and
from the head targeting you

4° **lomunculous of the frontal punc
and of the forceps whoring you**

he teeters to the stinking boss,
this arrogant capitalist
of limbo
swimming toward the regluing
of father-mother to the child sex organ
in order to drain the body entire,
entirely of its matter
and to put in its place, who?
The one whom being and nothingness
made,
as one gives to make peepee.

ET ILS, ONT TOUS FOUTU LE CAMP.

AND THEY, ALL GOT THE FUCK OUT.

Non, il reste la vrille affreuse,
la vrille-crime,
cette affreuse,
vieux clou, gendron,
déviation au profit du gendre faux
de la douleur sciée de l'os,

Ne voit-on pas que le gendre faux,
c'est Jizi-cri,
déjà connu au Mexique
bien avant sa fuite à Jérusalem sur un âne,
et le crucifiement d'Artaud au Golgotha.
Artaud
qui savait qu'il n'y a pas d'esprit
mais un corps
qui se refait comme l'engrenage du cadavre à dents,
dans la gangrène

du fémur
dedans.

No, there remains the ghastly gimlet,
the gimlet-crime,
this dreadful,
old nail, stud-in-law*,
deviation profiting the fake son-in-law
of the pain sawed from the bone,

Don't we see that the fake son-in-law,
it's Jizi-cry,
already known in Mexico
long before his flight to Jerusalem on an ass,
and the crucifying of Artaud at Golgotha.
Artaud
who knew that there was no spirit
but a body
that repairs itself like the gearing of a toothed
     cadaver,
in the gangrene

          of the thighbone
          within.

dakantala
dakis tekel
ta redaba
ta redabel
de stra muntils
o ept anis
o ept atra

de la douleur

                   suée

dans

                   l'os. —

Tout vrai langage
est incompréhensible,
comme la claque
du claque-dents ;
ou le claque (bordel)
du fémur à dents (en sang).

dakantala
dakis tekel
ta redaba
ta redabel
de stra muntils
o ept anis
o ept atra

of the pain

        sweated

in

        the bone. —

All' true language
is incomprehensible,
like the clap
of clapperdudgeons;
or the claptrap (cat house)
of the toothed thighbone (bloodied).

De la douleur minée de l'os
quelque chose naquit
qui devint ce qui fut esprit
pour décaper dans la douleur motrice,
de la douleur,
                cette matrice,
une matrice concrète

                et l'os,
                le fond du tuff
                qui devint os.

From the mined pain of the bone
something was born
which became that which spirit was
to scour in motory pain,
from the pain,
        this matrix,
a concrete matrix

      and the bone,
      the bedrock bottom
      which became bone.

MORALE

Ne te fatigue jamais plus qu'il ne faut, quitte à fonder une culture sur la fatigue de tes os.

MORAL

Don't tire yourself more than need be, even at
the price of founding a culture on the fatigue
of your bones.

MORALE

Quand le tuff fut mangé par l'os,
que l'esprit rongeait par derrière,
l'esprit ouvrit la bouche en trop
et il reçut dans le derrière
                    de la tête
un coup à dessécher ses os ;

            alors,

            ALORS,
            alors
            os par os
l'égalisation sempiternelle revint

**et tourna l'atome électrique
avant de fondre point par point.**

MORAL

When the bedrock was eaten by the bone,
that the spirit was gnawing from behind,
the spirit opened too much mouth
and received on the back
                of its head
a bone-withering blow;

            then,

            THEN,
            then
            bone by bone
the sempiternal equalization returned

and turned the electric atom
before point by point melting down.

CONCLUSION

Pour moi, simple
Antonin Artaud,
on ne me la fait pas à l'influence
quand on n'est qu'un homme
ou que
                dieu.

Je ne crois à ni père
                ni mère,

ja na pas
a papa-mama,

nature,
esprit
ou dieu,
satan
ou corps
ou être,
vie
ou néant,

rien qui soit dehors ou dedans
et surtout pas la bouche d'être,
trou d'un égout foré de dents
où se regarde tout le temps
l'homme qui tète sa substance

CONCLUSION

For me, simple
Antonin Artaud,
no one can bamboozle me with influence
when one is nothing but a man
or nothing but
                god.

I believe in neither father
                nor mother,

ain't gotta
daddy-mommy

nature,
spirit,
or god,
satan
or body
or being,
life
or nothingness,

nothing that is outside or inside
and above all not the mouth of being,
sewer hole drilled with teeth
where he's always watching himself
the man who sucks his substance

en moi,
pour me prendre un papa-maman,
et se refaire une existence
libre de moi
sur mon cadavre
ôté
du vide
même,

et reniflé
de temps
en temps.

Je dis
de par-dessus
le temps

comme si le temps
n'était pas frite,
n'était pas cette cuite frite
de tous les effrités
du seuil,
réembarqués dans leur cercueil.

in me,
to take a daddy-mommy from me,
and remake an existence
free of me
on my cadaver
removed
from the void
itself,

and sniffed
                    from time
                    to time.

I say
                    from above
                    time

as if time
were not a French fry,
were not this crocked fry
of all the friablized
of the threshold,
reembarked in their coffin.

NOTES BY CLAYTON ESHLEMAN

INDIAN CULTURE

OC XII, pp. 69–74. Originally published with *Here Lies* as a single book, by K editeur, in 1948, the two poems were both written on a single day, November 25, 1946. Both began in notebooks, and were subsequently dictated to Artaud's assistant, after which the poems were typed and corrected.

p. 9: "the pusseying father": "mimire" appears to be a coined, compound word, based on "mimi" (pussycat, and by extension the sexual "pussy"), and "mirer" (to take aim at, or to look closely at, to eye).

"the hollow mamuffin": "mamiche" also appears to be coined and compound, based on "mama" and "miche" (a round loaf of bread; in the plural, in the proper context, it can refer to buttocks). In the cases of "mimire" and "mimiche" we have sought to create compound words in English in which, as in the French, the end of one word is the beginning of the next.

"daddy-mommy": Probably the mundane "primal scene" as a caricature of the Father-Mother ("père-mère") conjunction, in Tibetan Buddhism known as Yab-Yum, transcendentally one of the manifestations of the Buddha. In the opening lines of the poem that follows *Indian Culture*, Artaud will suggest that the transcendental father-mother is merely a projection of daddy-mommy primal scene, which is embedded in his body. As the race of Amalakites are said to spring directly from the earth, and as the Tarahumaras "eat Peyote straight from the soil/while it is being born," so does Artaud, a parental system unto himself, bear his daughters directly from his own heart while he watches them being destroyed by forces committed to a sexual leveling of life.

"tusk holes": "boutis" is a rare word referring to the holes in fields made by boars rooting with their tusks.

HERE LIES

OC XII, pp. 75–100. Like the opening section of *Artaud the Mômo*, the opening section of *Here Lies* is heavily rhymed. Such rhyming, which falls in obsessive clusters rather than in any formal or conventional pattern, introduces a nursery-rhyme-like element into a visionary argument, giving a unique "veer" to the writing. We have refrained from attempting to match this rhyming because to do so plays havoc with the meaning.

p. 27: *"pantabazooms"'*: Artaud's *"falzourchte"* appears to be coined and augmented off "falzar," argot for trousers. The coined suffix recalls sounds that appeared in the chant ending "The Return of Artaud, the Mômo." Our word plays with pantaloons, linking it to a raffish word for big female breasts.

p. 29: "the viper (father life)": Artaud plays on "vipère" (viper) and, suggested by the "vie mère" (mother life) above it, "vie père" (father life).

p. 33: "scrubby grope slope/croupswarmed": "parpougnête" appears to be coined off "farfouiller," which conventionally means to rummage about, and erotically means to grope or fuck. The suffix is ironic, tender, and pejorative. "engruper" is also coined, and appears to be formed from such words as "agripper" (to clutch, seize), "agrouper" (to group) and "croup" (rump, croup, crupper etc.). Our thanks to Jean-Pierre Auxeméry and Daniel Delas for useful input here.

p. 39: "And that is how... all the sooners": For a brief but insightful commentary on this section, see Julia Kristeva's "l'Engendrement de la formule," *Tel quel* #38, 1969, pp. 58–59.

p. 43: "nolarking... titrating you": The passage is packed with word particles. We built our version off "alouette" (lark) which led us to "malarkey." We chose to keep the sound play of *"tirant" "titrant,"* forcing us to mistranslate *"tirant"* (shooting, or fucking).

p. 47: "stud-in-law": Based on Artaud's "gendron," which appears to be coined off "gendre" (son-in-law), to which an augmentative suffix has been added.

p. 49: *"All true language... (bloodied)"*: As a feminine noun, "claque" can refer to a slap, a claque (paid clappers), or kicking the bucket. A "claquedent" (in the text the hyphen is Artaud's) is a miserable wretch, a brothel, or a clapperdudgeon (a beggar born). "claque" as a masculine noun is an opera hat, or a brothel. By adding "bordel" to the line, Artaud signals that he prefers the cathouse meaning of the word here, so we play with "claptrap," conventionally a trick to gain applause or insincere sentiment, but in our version of Artaud heaven it is that trap in which one gets the clap.

Stephen Barber

Clayton Eshleman's Translation of Artaud's *Here Lies preceded by Indian Culture*

The two poetic works collected together here as *Here Lies preceded by Indian Culture* were created as a partly improvised vocal performance dictated during one session on 25 November 1946, based on provisional notes, and transcribed by Artaud's collaborator Paule Thévenin at Artaud's pavilion in Ivry-sur-Seine. The two works together form one of the outstanding experiments of Artaud's final period. Those two works were published in one volume in Paris on 20 January 1948 by the small poetry publisher K (also the envisaged publisher of Artaud's *Watchfiends and Rack Screams*), in an edition of 450 copies, at the moment immediately preceding the furore over the February 1948 censorship of Artaud's radio broadcast, *To have done with the judgement of god*; the privations of postwar Paris and paper shortages apparently led to the long interval between the completion of the works and their publication. (After Artaud's death, that publisher, K, directed by Henri Parisot and Alain Gheerbrandt, published a poetry magazine, also titled *K*, which, for its first issue in June 1948, collected many of Artaud's then-unknown final fragments, as a parallel publication to issue 5/6 of the poetry journal *84* which also published Artaud's last writings.) This DIAPHANES edition is the first time since 1948 that the two works, *Here Lies* and *Indian Culture*, have been published as Artaud intended, together as a single volume without other works.

Indian Culture is one of the first works of Artaud's last period, following his release from the asylum of Rodez in May 1946, to interrogate and re-envision his own corporeal history. It deals obliquely with his travels in Mexico in 1936 which Artaud had previously written about at that time and also at the asylum of Rodez; here, Artaud sets aside his previous preoccupations with peyote and the Tarahumara peoples' sorcerers (which he would return to in a final work on his Mexican journey and the Tarahumaras' rituals in February 1948) to directly anatomize his obsessions with gods, corporeality, and sexuality. Artaud's work appears expectorated as a sequence of livid curses, while being engulfed in a sensorial aura of reeks, agonies and splinterings.

Here Lies is Artaud's definitive declaration of autonomy for his own body from its birth to its imminent death, won at the cost of multiple battles against the infiltrating powers that he views as amassed to steal that birth and death away from him. The body may assert and exact its autonomy but that act also leaves it exposed to innumerable assaults and dangers from deities, beings and societies. Much of the imagery Artaud conjures in *Here Lies* – corporeal infiltrations, maleficent microbial proliferations, anatomical transmutation, and mutilated Incas – also constellates his drawings of that same moment; those drawings' edges also bear traces of the occasional glossolaliac eruptions that appear in *Here Lies*. Both works in this volume demonstrate Artaud's final poetry as a unique amalgam of delicate linguistic inventiveness and ferociously obscene invective.

*

Clayton Eshleman was born on 1 June 1935 in Indianapolis, Indiana, and died on the night of 29 January 2021 in Ypsilanti, Michigan. He had lived for lengthy periods in Kyoto,

Lima, Paris, Los Angeles and other cities, often to enable him to have access to the archives of the poets he was translating. Although he was an award-winning translator of the work of poets such as César Vallejo and Aimé Césaire, and produced many volumes of his own poetry, he is best known as the foremost English-language translator of the work of Artaud.

I met Eshleman in Paris in the mid 1990s at the moment when he was reaching the end of his three decades of work on his Artaud translations, though he would return to them in the early 2000s as new material was published. Eshleman travelled to Paris each summer to supervise a tour group on a journey through the cave systems of the Dordogne, lecturing to that audience on his own research into the cosmological belief systems of the prehistoric cave artists, eventually published as the book *Juniper Fuse* (2003). He was a very determined man and had been able to secure access to caves which were usually closed to visitors. I had been forewarned by people who had encountered him, such as the poet Anne Waldman, that Eshleman was an extremely irascible and argumentative man, and from my observations in Paris, that view seemed confirmed, though our joint interest in Artaud's work protected me from being the recipient of Eshleman's ire. He used his visits to Paris to meet Artaud's few surviving friends and collaborators, such as Florence Loeb, and we discussed translation issues around Artaud's multiply layered and glossolaliac writings prior to Eshleman's first publication of his assembled Artaud translations in 1995.

Eshleman was intensely interested in all religious beliefs and rituals, from those of Zen Buddhism to those of the Tarahumara peoples of northern Mexico whom Artaud visited in 1936; he was also keenly interested in shamanism, and in the apocalyptic revelations which preoccupied Artaud during his journey to Ireland in 1937. While I was living in Japan in 1997–98, I received many letters from Eshleman evoking his own years in Kyoto in the first half of the 1960s and his engagement with Zen

Buddhism in that era. He wrote about his many visits to temples in Kyoto, such as Daitoku-ji, often in the company of the poet Gary Snyder who was also living in Kyoto at that time, and expressed his desire to return to Japan and renew those studies. He told me that it was during his time in Kyoto that he had realized his vocation was to be a poet and translator, and he foresaw a return to Japan as a reactivation of that commitment. But, by then, he was working as a professor at a university in the Detroit area, and his duties there (source of much of his perpetual rage) prevented such a step.

In 2007–08, I met Eshleman frequently during a year when he was based as a visiting professor at UCLA. I was myself working in the Los Angeles area at the California Institute of the Arts, where Eshleman had himself worked in the late 1960s soon after that art school's foundation by Walt Disney and other benefactors. I invited Eshleman to make his first visit for forty years to CalArts to give a talk on his Artaud translations to the students, and he also evoked for them the wild atmosphere on the 1960s CalArts campus with his students habitually attending his seminars naked and telling him of their renunciation of all books. Several tutors at CalArts had been there from the beginning and recalled to me that, even in the late 1960s, Eshleman had been the fiercest and most belligerent person on campus. During many restaurant meals in Los Angeles, I quickly grew used to Eshleman's approach of invariably returning the food to the kitchen with a set of vitriolic protests. We also gave a joint reading at UCLA from our Artaud translations, and the audience's warm response to the event seemed to be a source of pleasure to Eshleman, who often asserted that he was an unknown figure whose work, despite his obsessional devotion to it, had passed the world by.

I was last in touch with Eshleman in 2019 to discuss this new DIAPHANES series of his Artaud translations, and though he expressed great enthusiasm for that opportunity for new attention for his translation work, he told me that, as a result of declining health, he had now ceased all activity in translation and poetry. Even so, collections of his own work such as *The Grindstone of Rapport: A Clayton Eshleman Reader* (2008) provide an aperture for readers to explore the depth of his own work, with its many engagements with worldwide belief systems, and their relationship to his work in translation.

Artaud's own engagement with religion had been an extremely fraught one. He was brought up as a Roman Catholic in Marseille in the first years of the twentieth century, but his family's background in Turkey and Greece also entailed encounters for him with Islam and Judaism. By the time of his involvement with the Surrealist movement in Paris in the mid 1920s, Artaud's position was adamantly atheistic. His apocalyptic manifestoes and travels of 1937 preceded his decade-long asylum incarceration during which he would oscillate between atheism and a return to a mystical form of Catholicism. It's conceivable that those religious oscillations were a response to the antithetical belief systems of the Rodez asylum doctors who were administering electroshock treatments to Artaud, which terrified him; the asylum director, Ferdière, was a lifelong militant atheist and anarchist, while his assistant, Latrémolière, was devoted to mystical theologies. To placate both doctors simultaneously was a high-wire act for Artaud.

In the final period of his life after his release from asylum incarceration, 1946–48, and through the body of writings which Eshleman translated, Artaud conducted a relentless combat against all religions, Christianity above all. That combat is reflected in the title of his radio broadcast for the French national radio station, *To have done with the judgement of god*. At the same time, Artaud contradictorily empathised with Christ's torture to the extent that he viewed Christ as his 'double' who had maliciously supplanted his own identity. Eshleman translated a passage of *Here Lies* as follows: '*Don't we see that the fake son-in-law,/it's Jizi-cry,/already known in Mexico/long before his* *flight to Jerusalem on an ass,/and the crucifying of Artaud at Golgotha./Artaud/who knew that there was no spirit/ but a body/that repairs itself like the gearing of a toothed cadaver,/in the gangrene/of the thighbone/*within.'

In order to render Artaud's anatomically charged and religiously contested poetry, Eshleman himself required both empathy and an immense knowledge of the multiple contestations at stake in Artaud's work. For that reason and many others, his life's work in translating Artaud's work (alongside other equally demanding poets) deserves enduring attention.

*

Eshleman's translations of Artaud's final period of work also served to refocus and transform the perception of that work for its English-language readership on their initial publications, and still do so, even more acutely, in DIAPHANES' new editions. Eshleman's translations, for the first time, present Artaud in English in an authentic form, rendered both with great creativity and erudition, and with an intricate and ferocious corporeality that matches Artaud's own. Eshleman translated Artaud with a comprehensive scholarly knowledge of the entirety of his work and of its multiple forms: the result of those three decades of sustained engagement.

Strangely, for a figure of Artaud's vast stature and influence, the English-language translations of his work over the past sixty or more years have never otherwise reached the affinitive and sensorial intensity that Eshleman achieved. From the first translation of Artaud in 1958, the Grove Press edition of *The Theatre and its Double* – and passing through Jack Hirschman's City Lights *Artaud Anthology* of 1965, the British publisher John Calder's volumes of 1968–74, Susan Sontag's edition of *Selected Writings* in 1976, and more recent publications – Artaud has often been banalized, sent askew, or has simply suffered the process of mis-representation he most feared and attacked. Hirschman's edition – a massive seller in the late 1960s, and the previous volume with a particular focus on Artaud's late work – demonstrates the combination of idiosyncrasy, misplaced enthusiasm and sheer ill-informedness that has often plagued English-language translations of Artaud. On receiving Hirschman's manuscript (the work of numerous translators) in 1964, its publisher, Lawrence Ferlinghetti, who had commissioned the anthology, wrote to Hirschman: 'I don't really understand how you operate... I do not understand your criteria for the *order*, or sequence, of the contents as a whole. It's not chronological, is it? What is it?'⁴; Artaud's collaborator Paule Thévenin complained in a letter to Ferlinghetti: 'The more deeply I look into the work Hirschman has done, the more furious I become... How on earth, to be frank about this, could you have put your trust in a person who doesn't speak a word of French and also doesn't understand a word of it?'². Even so, prior to Eshleman's translations, it was Hirschman's anthology that had provoked and actively perplexed – sometimes propelling them towards the original French – its hundreds of thousands of readers, such as Patti Smith and Anne Waldman, over several decades. Jack Hirschman died in San Francisco in 2021, the same year as Eshleman's death.

Since 1987, Artaud's drawings and notebooks have been exhibited many times, at Paris's Centre Georges Pompidou, New York's Museum of Modern Art, Vienna's Museum of Modern Art, and London's Cabinet Gallery, also transforming and realigning the perception of his work. The notebooks' curator at the Bibliothèque Nationale de France, Guillaume Fau, has accomplished invaluable work in making them accessible and in envisioning their eventual digitization. The series of events which I organized with the curator Matt Williams at Cabinet Gallery, Whitechapel Gallery and Visconti Studio in London in 2018 (marking the seventieth anniversary of Artaud's death and the end of decades of constrictive copyright controls and bitter feuds among Artaud's heirs) accentuated the immense and interconnected span of Artaud's work: poetry, sound, film, art. This DIAPHANES series embodies that same aim of projecting the infinite span and profound strata of Artaud's work, evident most tangibly in its last moments, and for English-language readers in Eshleman's superb translations.

NOTES

1   Ferlinghetti, *Letter of 17 February 1964*, unpublished, collection of the Doheny Library, USC, Los Angeles.

2   Paule Thévenin, *Letter of 20 November 1965*, unpublished, collection of the Doheny Library, USC, Los Angeles.

CONTENTS

© DIAPHANES 2021
ISBN 978-3-0358-0364-8

DIAPHANES
LIMMATSTRASSE. 270 | CH-8005 ZURICH
DRESDENER STR. 118 | D-10999 BERLIN
57 RUE DE LA ROQUETTE | F-75011 PARIS

PRINTED IN GERMANY
LAYOUT: 2EDIT, ZURICH

WWW.DIAPHANES.NET